AMAZING WONDERS

GREAT WALL OF CHINA

BY MATT LILLEY

CREATIVE EDUCATION • CREATIVE PAPERBACKS

Published by Creative Education and Creative Paperbacks
P.O. Box 227, Mankato, Minnesota 56002
Creative Education and Creative Paperbacks
are imprints of The Creative Company
www.thecreativecompany.us

Design by The Design Lab
Art direction by Graham Morgan
Edited by Jill Kalz

Images by Getty (Andrew Benton/Construction Photography/Avalon), Pexels (Alex Qian, Markus Winkler, Ridzuan Ibrahim, TonyNojmanSK), Unsplash (Joel Danielson, Max van den Oetelaar, Rafik Wahba, Robert Nyman, Usukhbayar Gankhuyag, Vincent Guth), Wikimedia Commons

Library of Congress Cataloging-in-Publication Data
Names: Lilley, Matt, author.
Title: Great Wall of China / Matt Lilley.
Description: Mankato, MN : Creative Education and Creative Paperbacks, [2025] | Series: Amazing wonders | Includes bibliographical references and index. | Audience: Ages 6–9 | Audience: Grades 2–3 | Summary: "An elementary-level introduction to the Great Wall of China, covering how, when, and why the famous ancient wonder was built. Includes captions, on-page definitions, additional resources, and an index"—Provided by publisher.
Identifiers: LCCN 2023042440 (print) | LCCN 2023042441 (ebook) | ISBN 9781640268593 (library binding) | ISBN 9781682774090 (paperback) | ISBN 9798889890218 (ebook)
Subjects: LCSH: Great Wall of China (China)—Juvenile literature. | China—History—To 221 B.C.—Juvenile literature. | Walls—China—Design and construction—History—Juvenile literature.
Classification: LCC DS793.G67 L545 2025 (print) | LCC DS793.G67 (ebook) | DDC 931—dc23/eng/20230921
LC record available at https://lccn.loc.gov/2023042440
LC ebook record available at https://lccn.loc.gov/2023042441

Printed in China

Table of Contents

The Great Wall is more than 5,000 miles (8,047 kilometers) long. It stretches across northern China. It is not one wall, though. It is made of many parts.

The wall is nicknamed the "Sleeping Dragon" because of its long, snakelike shape.

Long ago, soldiers sent signals from the tall towers with flags, smoke, and fire.

The Great Wall

runs mostly east and west. It divides fertile land in the south from dry grassland in the north. One end stands in the Bohai Sea. The other is in the Gobi Desert.

fertile capable of growing lots of plants

Emperor Qin ruled until 210 BC, when he died at age 49.

The Great Wall

started with a few **sections**. They were built between 600 and 300 BC. The first leader of China, Emperor Qin Shi Huang, had these sections connected around 215 BC. Most of this first wall is gone now.

sections parts of a whole

姓嬴名政始自始皇乙卯即王位庚辰併天下稱皇帝
在位三十七年居王位二十五年即帝位十二年壽五十

Northern China is very cold and often snowy in winter.

The wall was meant to unify the people of China. It was also meant to keep them safe. Nomads often attacked from the north. In the 1200s, Genghis Khan and his Mongol warriors got past the wall. They took over the country.

nomads people who travel from place to place; wanderers

unify to bring together

The Mongols ruled China for more than 100 years. Then, in 1368, the Ming Dynasty (1368–1644) drove them back out. But future attacks were likely. So the Ming people made the wall bigger than ever.

The Mongol empire of Genghis Khan stretched from the Pacific Ocean to Europe.

Much of the Great Wall was built with bricks and earth. Workers laid the bricks in two rows. They filled the space between the rows with earth. Then they tightly pressed the earth, making it hard and strong.

Solid construction has kept the wall standing for hundreds of years.

Building atop steep hills and mountains was dangerous work.

The wall is made of millions of bricks. Workers set the bricks by hand. They used **mortar** to hold them in place. Workers often added sticky rice to the mortar to make it stronger.

mortar a glue that holds building units together

Palace from the Ming Dynasty

The Great Wall is the longest structure made by people. No one knows exactly how long it is. Some parts are falling. Others have disappeared. Most of the wall that people see today was built during the Ming Dynasty.

Much of the Great Wall was also a road.

China's early rulers built the Great Wall to keep people out. Today, the wall brings people in. Millions of visitors go to the wall every year. To many, it is a celebration of China's history and culture.

Many local people visit the wall during Chinese holidays.

Wonder Spotlight: Drinking Dragon

Shanhai Pass is the easternmost section of the Great Wall. It was built during the Ming Dynasty. Part of the pass reaches into the Bohai Sea. This part is called "Old Dragon's Head." It looks like the head and long snout of a dragon taking a drink of water! The head is also a watchtower.

Read More

Jackson, Tom. *Wonders of the World.* New York, N.Y.: DK Publishing, 2022.

Noll, Elizabeth. *The Great Wall of China.* Minneapolis: Bellwether Media, 2021.

Spanier, Kristine. *Great Wall of China.* Minneapolis: Jump!, 2021.

Websites

KidzSearch Encyclopedia: Great Wall of China
https://wiki.kidzsearch.com/wiki/Great_Wall_of_China
Learn about construction of the Great Wall.

National Geographic Kids: China
https://kids.nationalgeographic.com/geography/countries/article/china
Discover facts about China's land, people, and more.

Index